To: ....

From: ....

MR. MEN   LITTLE MISS
by Roger Hargreaves

GROSSET & DUNLAP
Penguin Young Readers Group
An Imprint of Penguin Random House LLC

All rights reserved. Previously published in 2017 by Egmont UK Limited
as *My Daddy*. Published in the United States of America in 2019 by Grosset & Dunlap,
an imprint of Penguin Random House LLC, 345 Hudson Street, New York, New York 10014.
GROSSET & DUNLAP is a trademark of Penguin Random House LLC. Manufactured in China.

www.mrmen.com

ISBN 9781524792374   10 9 8 7 6 5 4 3

MY DAD
and me
by Roger Hargreaves

Grosset & Dunlap
An Imprint of Penguin Random House

My dad is full of fun from the moment he wakes up.

He is as silly as Mr. Funny
and makes the best faces.

My dad can do the most impossible things.

And sometimes he can even make my dreams come true.

...and as strong as Mr. Strong.

He is the fastest thing on two legs.

And he can eat the most enormous plates of food.

My dad is very smart and knows lots of things.

But he can't always
do everything
he tries.

He reads stories in the loudest, funniest voices.

And I can even hear him
when he's sleeping.

My dad can sometimes be a bit grumpy, just like me.

But he's always
there to help me.

He has his very own style . . .

. . . and sometimes likes things to be just so.

But my dad is so much fun and can make anyone smile . . .

... especially when he tells his silly jokes.

We do the coolest
things together.

But he also likes his quiet time.

My dad is full of mischief.

And you have to watch out for his tickles.

Life with Dad is one big adventure.

I think he might have even met Santa Claus.

When I'm happy, it makes him happy, too.

My dad is the best dad
in the whole world.

I love my dad
and he loves me.

MY DAD

My dad is most like **MR.** ....

I love it when my dad reads ....

.... to me.

My dad makes me laugh when ....

....

He always knows when ....

....

My dad is very silly because ....

....

My dad is lots of fun and likes ....

Our favorite thing to do together is ....

I know he loves me when ....

My dad's tickles are the best because ....

....

This is a picture
of my dad:

by ....

age ....